Princess Ponies

The Special Secret

The Princess Ponies series

A Magical Friend
A Dream Come True
The Special Secret
A Unicorn Adventure!

☆ Coming soon ☆

An Amazing Rescue
Best Friends Forever!

Princess Ponies

The Special Secret

CHLOE RYDER

BLOOMSBURY

NEW YORK   LONDON   NEW DELHI   SYDNEY

First published in Great Britain in June 2013 by Bloomsbury Publishing Plc
Published in the United States of America in August 2014
by Bloomsbury Children's Books
www.bloomsbury.com

Bloomsbury is a registered trademark of Bloomsbury Publishing Plc

For information about permission to reproduce selections from this book, write to
Permissions, Bloomsbury Children's Books, 1385 Broadway, New York, New York 10018
Bloomsbury books may be purchased for business or promotional use. For information on
bulk purchases please contact Macmillan Corporate and Premium Sales Department at
specialmarkets@macmillan.com

Library of Congress Cataloging-in-Publication Data
Ryder, Chloe.
The special secret / Chloe Ryder.
pages   cm.   — (Princess ponies ; 3)
Summary: On Harvest Day, Pippa and her princess pony friend Stardust
head to the Grasslands to help—and to search for the remaining missing
horseshoes needed to save the enchanted island of Chevalia.
ISBN 978-1-61963-237-0 (paperback) • ISBN 978-1-61963-238-7 (e-book)
[1. Ponies—Fiction. 2. Magic—Fiction. 3. Princesses—Fiction.
4. Harvest festivals—Fiction.] I. Title.
PZ7.R95898Sp 2014   [Fic]—dc23   2013048653

Typeset by Hewer Text UK Ltd, Edinburgh
Printed in China by Leo Paper Products, Heshan, Guangdong
2 4 6 8 10 9 7 5 3

For Sidonie, a true pony lover

With special thanks to Julie Sykes

The Pony

Queen
Moonshine

Princess
Crystal

Princess
Cloud

Princess
Stardust

Princess
Honey

Royal Family

King
Firestar

Prince
Jet

Prince
Comet

Prince
Storm

Cloud
Forest

Volcano

Wild Forest

Stableside
Castle

Chevalia

Horseshoe Hills

Savannah

Grasslands

Canter's Prep School

The Fields

Mane Street

Early one morning, just before dawn, two ponies stood in an ancient court-yard, looking sadly at a stone wall.

"In all my life this wall has never been empty. I can't believe that the horse-shoes have been taken—and just before Midsummer Day too," said the stallion.

He was a handsome animal—a copper-colored pony, with strong legs and bright eyes, dressed in a royal red sash.

The mare was a dainty yet majestic palomino with a golden coat and a pure white tail that fell to the ground like a waterfall.

She whinnied softly. "We don't have much time to find them all."

With growing sadness the two ponies watched the night fade away and the sun rise. When the first ray of sunlight spread into the courtyard it lit up the wall, showing the imprints where the golden horseshoes should have been hanging.

"Midsummer Day is the longest day of the year," said the stallion quietly. "It's the time when our ancient horse-shoes must renew their magical energy. If the horseshoes are still missing in eight days, then by nightfall on the

3

eighth day, their magic will fade and our beautiful island will be no more."

Sighing heavily, he touched his nose to his queen's.

"Only a miracle can save us now," he said.

The queen dipped her head, the diamonds on her crown sparkling in the early morning light.

"Have faith," she said gently. "I sense that a miracle is coming."

Chapter 1

"Look how blue the sky is this morning," said Pippa MacDonald. She was admiring the pretty view of the island from a window high up in Stableside Castle.

"It's always lovely here on Chevalia," Princess Stardust said, carefully braiding red ribbons into her long white mane.

It might not be if you don't hurry up, Pippa thought.

It wasn't Stardust's fault that as a princess pony, and seventh in line to the throne, she was expected to always look her best. And it certainly wasn't Stardust's fault that the island of Chevalia was in danger.

Pippa picked up a comb and started brushing Stardust's tail. It was so long it hung down to the floor and Pippa had to kneel to reach it. She could still hardly believe that, while on vacation with her family, she'd been brought to Chevalia, a magical island where ponies can talk. Pippa had discovered that Chevalia was in grave danger. The eight golden horseshoes that gave life to the island had been stolen from the ancient wall in the castle courtyard. If they weren't all back in their places on Midsummer Day, so that they could have their magical energy renewed by the Midsummer sun, then Chevalia would fade away.

With Stardust's help Pippa had already found two horseshoes, but now there were just four days until Midsummer, and six horseshoes were still missing.

Placing the comb on the dresser, Pippa stood back to admire her work. Then she put on the pretty dress that had magically appeared overnight and was neatly laid out for her on a chair.

"Can we search the Horseshoe Hills today?" she asked.

"But it's Harvest Day," Stardust said, studying her reflection in a long mirror.

7

"Everyone who attends Canter's Prep School for Fine Equine is expected to go to the Grasslands to bring the harvest home. That includes me."

"Oh!" Pippa's heart sank.

Even though Chevalia was under threat, Stardust's parents, Queen Moonshine and King Firestar, were determined that the Royal Family continue their many traditions so as not to worry everyone.

"Harvest Day is fun," Stardust assured her. "And it's not all work. The best part is the picnic lunch—it's like a party with all our favorite things to eat, like carrots dipped in linseed oil."

"I suppose we haven't searched the Grasslands yet," said Pippa.

"Then we'll do it today while we're helping with the harvest," Stardust said decisively.

Pippa wasn't sure how much searching they would have time for if they were expected to work, but it was better than nothing.

"Let's go then," she said, eager to get started.

☆

After a quick breakfast in the castle's huge dining room, Pippa, Stardust, and the four of her brothers and sisters who still attended Canter's Prep School followed their nanny, Mrs. Steeplechase, down to the Grasslands.

"Stop it," Pippa whispered, trying

not to giggle as Stardust imitated the way her teacher waddled.

"No talking!" Mrs. Steeplechase said, turning around to glare at them.

"Sorry," said Pippa. She turned her attention to the lines of ponies who were approaching the Grasslands from every direction. There were lots of

foals, their manes and tails braided with purple ribbons, trotting beside their parents.

"They're from Canter's Nursery School," Stardust explained. "The babies wear purple ribbons, the toddlers wear red ribbons like me, and the older kids wear blue ones. We should have braided ribbons in your hair too. When we get to the Grasslands, I'll ask if anyone has any extra ribbon so you're not left out."

"Thanks," Pippa said absently, her mind on the missing horseshoes. She really hoped that they would find at least one today.

The Grasslands were going to be difficult to search. The grass grew so tall that in places it was higher than Pippa's head. It was like walking through a pale-green forest. Soon they came out of the grass and into a clearing. To Pippa's surprise there was a small farmhouse with a large yard.

"Mucker!" squealed Stardust. Breaking away from the group, she trotted over to a stocky dark-brown pony with a white blaze, four white stockings, and a black mane and tail.

"Princess Stardust!"

Stardust and Mucker brushed noses.

"I'm so glad you've come to help with the harvest. I've heard lots about you," he added, shyly nodding at Pippa. "You're here to save Chevalia."

Pippa blushed as red as a strawberry.

Everyone had such high hopes for her. She didn't want to let Chevalia down.

Stardust's big sister, Princess Crystal, was standing in the middle of the farm-yard putting ponies into groups. As first in line to the throne of Chevalia, she was expected to help supervise the younger ponies on Harvest Day.

"No talking!" Crystal yelled as she looked at her clipboard. "Stardust and Pippa, you're with—eeek!"

Crystal let out a huge shriek and, dropping her clipboard, galloped full speed across the yard.

Stardust snorted with laughter, then quickly turned it into a cough as Crystal trotted back, her nose in the air as if nothing had happened.

"It was a horsefly," Stardust explained to a puzzled Pippa. "Crystal's terrified of them."

Crystal nervously batted the air with her clipboard in case the horsefly returned. She continued, "Stardust and Pippa are with Mucker."

Mucker's face lit up. "Come on—I'll

show you both where to go," he said happily.

Mucker led them out of the yard to a muddy field full of tall grass with stems as thick as bamboo shoots. A group of ponies wearing red ribbons were already hard at work. Their legs

and faces were splattered with mud and their coats were steaming. As Pippa and Stardust trotted over to the group with Mucker, he explained that it was very hard work harvesting the grass.

"It's much thicker than usual," said Mucker. "Dad can't understand it. He didn't do anything different this year."

The members of Mucker's family were farm ponies, and he loved working with them on the land. He gave Pippa some tools and showed her how to harvest the grass.

Pippa learned quickly and realized that she was beginning to enjoy the work. The grass may have been thick and strong but it made a soft, whispery noise as it was cut.

The whispering grew more insistent. Suddenly, Pippa realized it was a voice.

"What did you say?" she asked Stardust.

"Nothing," replied Stardust, who had a smudge of brown mud on her face.

Pippa was puzzled—she was sure

Stardust had said something. She continued cutting and after a while she heard Stardust speak again.

"Sorry, I didn't quite catch that," Pippa said.

"Catch what?" asked Stardust.

"What you just said."

Stardust looked strangely at Pippa. "I never said a word."

"But I can hear a voice. Listen!" Pippa added. "There it is again."

Stardust stood still, her ears twitching as she concentrated on listening. "Sorry," she said at last. "All I can hear is the buzz of horseflies, nothing else."

Pippa couldn't understand it. The buzzing voice was beginning to irritate her. Why couldn't Stardust hear it too?

"Well, look who it is," a voice said loudly—a different voice, but one that Pippa knew. "It's Princess Grunge and her best friend, Dirt Girl!"

Pippa turned around and faced Cinders, the meanest pony in the Royal Court.

Chapter 2

"So now we know," Cinders said loudly, her eyes narrowing.

"Know what?" asked Stardust.

"That you're a fake." Cinders gave a high-pitched laugh. "You can't be a princess because a real princess would never get her hooves dirty. You're just an ordinary farm pony like Mucker."

"Of course I'm a real princess," Stardust said angrily.

"No, you're not," Cinders replied. "That's what my mom says anyway."

With that, Cinders swept past Stardust, taking great care not to step in the mud.

Stardust's brown eyes glittered with tears. "What did she mean?" she asked.

"Ignore her," Pippa said, stroking

Stardust's mud-splattered nose. "She was just being nasty to upset you."

"Are you sure?"

"Yes," Pippa said, even though she wasn't convinced. Cinders had sounded threatening and as if she knew something, but Pippa didn't want to frighten Stardust. She continued to stroke her nose, until she stopped shaking and calmed down.

"Cinders is right, though," Stardust said at last. "If I have to help with the harvest, then I should be given a cleaner job."

Mucker let out a snort of surprise. "Getting dirty has never bothered you before. We've always had a lot of fun together on the farm."

"Not anymore," Stardust said firmly. "It's time I started acting like a real princess."

To Mucker's dismay, Stardust flatly refused to help further. Instead she tore up some grass and used it to wipe the mud from her face, legs, and hooves.

"I'm going to ask Crystal for something else to do," she announced. "Something cleaner and more worthy of a princess pony." And she trotted off.

"I'll never get to see Stardust if she stops visiting the farm," Mucker said sadly. "I'd love to visit her at the castle but that's not going to happen—not when I come from a farming family. Besides, I'm too busy with farmwork to attend the Royal Court."

Pippa started to go after Stardust but quickly changed her mind. Poor Mucker was so upset—she couldn't leave him now. Keeping one eye on Stardust, she continued to help with the harvest while also keeping a lookout for shiny objects in the mud.

It was a long, hard morning. Pippa's back ached and her hands grew sore from gripping her tools and from all the cutting work. In the distance she could see that Stardust wasn't making much progress with her new job of collecting the cut grass. A cloud of horseflies was buzzing around her head, and each time Stardust swatted them away with her tail they just flew at her again.

"Go away, you awful things," Stardust shouted, angrily stomping a hoof.

The horseflies were becoming even more agitated. Buzzing loudly, they flew in circles around Stardust's head. Pippa ran over to see if she could help. But after swatting repeatedly at the horse-flies with her hands, she realized that it wasn't making any difference. She stood still and listened. The horseflies were making the same funny buzzing noise, like whispery voices, that she'd heard earlier. She decided to try something.

"Anyone would think that the horseflies were trying to talk to you," Pippa said.

Stardust stopped being cross and whinnied with laughter. "Talking horseflies? That's crazy!" she exclaimed. "That's the funniest thing I've heard all morning. Oh, look—there's Mucker's older brother, Trojan. He helps run the farm with Mucker's dad. He must have come to check on us. Let's say hello."

"Wait," Pippa said, still trying to figure out if she was imagining things or if the horseflies really were trying to tell them something.

But Stardust was already on her way over to the two brothers. Pippa followed.

"Hi, Trojan. Have you come to help or are you here to boss us around like Crystal?" she asked.

Trojan blushed at the mention of Crystal.

"Mucker and I were just discussing the best way to harvest the grass," he said gruffly. "But if Crystal's here I'm sure everything is under control."

Trojan's dark-brown coat still looked ruddy as he hurried away.

"Did I say the wrong thing?" asked Stardust.

"Well, Trojan really likes Crystal, but she barely notices him," Mucker explained. "Don't say I told you that, though!"

Stardust giggled. "Poor Trojan, liking my bossy big sister!"

"I think we should get back to work," Mucker said.

"He's right," Pippa said. "The Grasslands are so much bigger than I expected. We're never going to get all the harvest in *and* look for horseshoes in one day."

"It doesn't matter if the harvesting isn't finished today, but we do have to find the horseshoes quickly," Stardust said thoughtfully. "Let's go down to the stream—we haven't searched that area yet. The grass is much shorter near the stream, and we can have our picnic lunch there too."

"But I haven't finished looking here," said Pippa.

"We can come back later," Stardust replied.

"We should finish searching this area first," Pippa said firmly. "We should search each area properly before we move on to the next one; otherwise we might miss something."

A mixture of emotions flashed across Stardust's face, but at last she said, "You're right, Pippa. I'm so glad you're here to help—I'm definitely not as organized as you are. Let's search this part of the Grasslands thoroughly before lunch."

Pippa and Stardust slowly moved away from their harvesting group and put their efforts into searching for the horseshoes.

"We shouldn't make it too obvious that we've stopped harvesting," Stardust said quietly. "Remember that Mom and Dad want us to carry on as normal so we don't frighten anyone."

Every now and then Pippa heard Cinders's voice across the field. She was even bossier than Crystal, ordering the younger ponies around and avoiding getting her own hooves dirty.

"Anyone would think *her* mom was the queen and not jusssst a baronesssss," a tiny voice buzzed in her ear.

Pippa jumped with surprise. "Who's

that?" she asked, searching around the field.

"Mmmmeeee," hummed the voice.

Thinking she must be imagining things, Pippa tapped her ear with her hand.

"Careful! You nearly sssswatted meee."

A large horsefly darted in front of Pippa and hovered by her nose. She blinked in amazement.

"You!" she exclaimed. "Was that you talking to me?"

"Yesssss. My name is Zimb. Weeee've been trying to talk to Princess Star-dust all morning but she just won't lisssssssten," he said, waving his three friends over.

"We neeeeed help," the horseflies

said. "Pleasssse say that you'll help ussss or we're all going to be in great danger."

Chapter 3

"Two ponies came to see us out here on the Grasslands," explained Zimb, the largest of the horseflies. "They told us the Mistresssss had sent them on behalf of every pony in Chevalia because she wants to make peace with us and to be friendsss forever. They gave us two golden horseshoesss to prove they meant what they said. We were ssso excited. We've been trying to make friendsssss with the ponies for ages. But then we learned that the golden horse-shoesss had been stolen and that this put Chevalia in serious danger. The Mistresssss tricked us."

The Mistress! Pippa had no idea who she was, but each time they came close to finding a horseshoe her name came up. Pippa wondered whether this mysterious Mistress was behind the disappearance of all the horseshoes.

"Who is this Mistress?" she asked.

"You know, the hooded pony with the big cloak," the horseflies said excitedly.

As Pippa was taking this in, the horseflies continued, "We wanted to return the horseshoesss to the king and queen but we can't find the place where we left them. The grassss has grown too long. Can you help ussss?"

Something clicked in Pippa's head.

"That's it!" she cried. "So there are definitely two horseshoes here in the Grasslands."

She quickly ran to Stardust and filled her in on what the horseflies had told her, adding, "That's why the grass has grown so long—it's because of the magic from the two horseshoes."

Stardust was amazed but she was even more surprised that Pippa had heard the horseflies talking.

"I had no idea that horseflies could speak!" she whinnied. "But then I've never really listened to their buzzing."

As Stardust and Pippa set about

finding the two horseshoes, they grew hungry and even more tired. When they stopped for a short break, Pippa had a thought.

"If the magic from the horseshoes has made the grass grow taller than normal, then they must be buried where the grass is longest."

"Of course!" exclaimed Stardust. She nuzzled Pippa's arm. "You're so clever."

"You're clever too," Pippa said modestly.

Stardust turned pink with delight. Puffing out her chest, she said, "Let's go and ask Mucker where the longest grass is. He knows these fields like the back of his hoof!"

"Good idea," said Pippa.

They found Mucker with a group of ponies close to the stream and asked him where the longest grass was.

"Over there," Mucker said, pointing toward the water. "It's very muddy, though."

"I don't mind," said Pippa. She ran over to the stream and along the bank until she found an enormous clump of grass stretching high above her head. The ground was boggy and squishy. Pippa was glad her dress didn't have long sleeves as she sank her hands into the mud.

"Ew!" Stardust said, turning up her nose. "Careful, Pippa—you're getting mud everywhere!"

Pippa was too busy scooping up

handfuls of mud to hear Stardu...
only when a deep voice boome...
"What are you doing?" that she stopp...
digging.

"King Firestar." Pippa's face felt hot
as she dropped him a curtsy. "We think
two of the missing horseshoes might be
buried here."

"Hmmm." The king looked at Stardust and he stared at her for a long time. "Let me tell you a story," he said at last. "I was a farm pony once. My family—your grandparents, Stardust—owned a huge farm and everyone had to help out. I remember one Harvest Day in particular, when it had rained for weeks and the fields were even muddier than these are now." King Firestar poked the ground with his hoof and watched as black mud oozed over it. "Harvesting in the mud was fun, but there was one little pony who didn't think so. She was a pretty palomino princess. At first she was very prim and proper, standing with her hooves neatly together and refusing to help. But after a while she saw how much fun everyone was having. Fed up with being left out, she joined in the harvesting, and to her surprise she loved it. Her beautiful coat was covered in mud by the time the harvest was done but the princess didn't care. She just jumped in the stream to clean herself off. I fell in love with that princess pony and I've loved her ever since."

"Stop it! You're embarrassing me," said another familiar voice. "Besides, you tell that story every year."

"Your Majesty," Pippa said, curtsying.

"How is the harvest coming along?" the queen asked, her magnificent palomino coat gleaming in the sunlight. "Is everyone working hard?"

41

Mucker stepped forward. "Yes, Your Majesty," he said, too loyal to give Stardust away.

Stardust hung her head in shame. "I think I could work harder," she mumbled.

"Don't let us stop you then," said the queen. "There's enough time to do a bit more before lunch."

As the queen and king moved away, Stardust began to dig in the mud. Soon she was muddy up to her knees, but her dirt-stained face glowed with happiness.

"Dad was right. This is really fun," she said, kicking up more mud. "Look at Crystal and Trojan over there. Wouldn't it be fun if they followed in Mom and Dad's hoofsteps and got married?"

"Ssssh!" Pippa giggled. "You're not supposed to say anything about that."

"Who's getting married?" Crystal called, trotting over. "And what are you doing digging around in the mud, Stardust?"

Stardust tried not to giggle. "We're looking for missing horseshoes," she replied, and then quickly told her what the horseflies had said.

"Well, don't let me hold you up," Crystal said, walking off to check on another group of ponies who were working nearby.

☆

Just before they stopped for lunch, there was a light rain shower, which made the ground even muddier.

"Look at Cinders," Pippa said, as she watched the pony take cover in the barn.

"She's done even less work than me," said Stardust.

"But she's having less fun than you," commented Pippa, who loved the feel of the mud and didn't care how dirty she got. "Ouch! What was that?"

Her heart skipped a beat as her fingers touched something cold. Pippa frantically scooped away the mud under her. It was up to her elbows but she hardly noticed it. She was on to something! She could feel the magic tingling in her fingers as they scraped away at the object buried in the sticky ground.

"I'm almost there," Pippa panted, while Stardust watched anxiously.

Wrapping her fingers around her find, Pippa pulled. But the object was stuck.

"Let me help," Stardust said, gently taking the hem of Pippa's dress in her mouth so that she could pull her backward.

"One, two, three, *pull!*" yelled Pippa.

There was a loud noise, like water being sucked down a drain, then she and Stardust fell back as the object was suddenly worked free. They landed in an enormous patch of mud.

"Yes!" Pippa shouted, holding up the object in delight. "It's a very dirty golden horseshoe!"

"Hooray!" Stardust cheered, scrambling up onto her legs. "That's three horseshoes we've found now. And there's another one here somewhere. . . ."

Just then a gong sounded.

"Lunchtime," Stardust said. "Let's eat before we look for the fourth one."

"We should hang this horseshoe on the Whispering Wall first," Pippa said, even though she was famished.

"Let's eat first," said Stardust.

"But—" Pippa started to argue.

"We need to keep our strength up," Stardust said firmly. "Besides, taking one horseshoe back to the castle will waste too much time. Let's wait until we've found both of them."

"Okay," Pippa said reluctantly, but she knew that Stardust had a point.

She rinsed the horseshoe in the stream and cleaned away the dirt until it glittered. Then they made their way over to the huge portable troughs that were set out for lunch.

"When we find the other horse-shoe, we'll have found half of them," Pippa said.

"Oh!" Stardust exclaimed, her eyes shining with hope. "Then let's hurry up and eat lunch so we can find it!"

Chapter 4

The picnic was noisy and fun. Canter's ponies and all the farming ponies were covered in mud, their coats were matted, and their school ribbons were soaked and unraveling—but they were all relishing Harvest Day.

Only Cinders still looked neat—her chestnut coat shone, and her braided mane and tail were still held neatly in place with shiny red ribbons.

"Look at the state of you all," she said, wrinkling her nose.

No one was listening, though. They were too busy telling stories about their morning and admiring the golden horseshoe that Stardust and Pippa had propped on a tree at the picnic site. Pippa was still a little worried that they hadn't taken the horseshoe back to the castle, and she mentioned her concerns to Stardust.

"Don't worry, the horseshoe will be fine," the princess pony said. "There are plenty of ponies around to look after it, and it would have been a shame to miss the picnic lunch."

Pippa had to agree. The castle's serving ponies had sent her a special packed

lunch that included a peanut butter and jelly sandwich, carrot sticks, strawberries, and a whole jug of fizzy peach juice. Everything looked delicious and it would be a pity to waste it.

"Okay, but when we go back to work, we should ask a pony to guard the horseshoe for us."

"Good idea," Stardust said, lowering her head into a trough of honeyed oats.

They were just finishing lunch when a swarm of horseflies flew at Stardust. The ponies next to her whinnied in alarm and Mucker trotted over, his head down.

"Get out of here, you pesky beasts," he snorted.

"Wait!" buzzed the horseflies. "We want to talk to the princess."

Mucker was about to charge at them but Stardust shouted, "Mucker, stop! Don't hurt them. They're my friends."

"Thank you, princess," Zimb said.

"You can talk to the horseflies?" Mucker's eyes nearly popped out of his head.

"It's easy. Pippa showed me how," said Stardust. "All you have to do is listen very carefully."

By now the rest of Canter's had stopped eating and were listening too. The nursery school foals were so in awe that they couldn't stop looking at Stardust. The only pony not impressed was Cinders.

"If you think I'm going to listen to a horsefly, think again," she snorted. "They're nothing but nasty pests. Ouch!" Cinders let out a neigh and started dancing around in irritation.

"Ssssorry," buzzed Zimb. "I didn't mean to bite you on the bottom. I tripped by accident. Honestly, I did!"

He sounded so insincere that Stardust burst out laughing. Cinders scowled and marched away angrily. Pippa bit her lip to stop herself from giggling. Even though Cinders was so unpleasant, she still felt a little bit sorry for her.

"We sssssaw that you found one of the horseshoesssss," buzzed Zimb.

"Yes," Stardust said. "And how did you do?"

54

"We found nothing," Zimb said sadly, "but we'll keep looking now we know how important it is to have all eight horseshoes back on the ancient wall in time for Midsummer Day. We're just sssssssorry that by accepting two of them from the Mistress we caused ssssso much trouble."

"It's not your fault. And thanks for all your help," Stardust said gratefully.

Pippa was deep in thought. Who was the Mistress? The question still bothered her. She looked up and noticed Cinders, who was lying on the ground by herself looking very sad and lonely. Pippa couldn't help but feel sorry for her, and she wandered over to her.

"Please, will you look after this horseshoe for us while we search for the other one?" Pippa asked.

Cinders looked very surprised, but she agreed. "All right," she said.

"Why did you ask her that?" Stardust whispered angrily when Pippa rejoined her. "She doesn't deserve such a special job. She's done nothing all morning."

Pippa shrugged. "Mom says you should always give people a chance to be nice. If we're kind to Cinders, then maybe she'll start being kind back."

Stardust nuzzled Pippa's arm with her nose. "Your mom sounds nice," she said.

"She is," Pippa said, feeling a little homesick. But at least Mom and her

brother and sister wouldn't be missing her—Chevalia existed in a special
time bubble so that Pippa could stay
there for as long as she needed,
while time stood still in her own world.
She pushed the sad feeling away. "Let's
get started," she said.

Pippa and Stardust searched and
searched, until their fingers and hooves
were sore from digging through the
mud and dirt and grass.

It was late afternoon when Pippa said
wearily, "Let's stop for a drink."

"Good idea." Stardust straightened
up. She started to walk back to the
stream, where there was a drinking

trough with fresh running water, but she slipped on a patch of mud.

"Careful!" said Pippa.

"Ouch!" Stardust whinnied. "I stubbed my hoof on something hard."

Her eyes met Pippa's and they stared at each other for a split second. Then, wordlessly, they threw themselves to the ground and began scraping the mud away. Pippa's fingers touched something hard and cold. Her heart thudded with excitement. Could it be the other horseshoe that was missing in the Grasslands?

"We've found the fourth missing horseshoe!" squealed Stardust.

"Isn't it funny how sometimes you just stumble across the exact thing that you're trying so hard to find!" said Pippa, delighted. "How lucky!"

"Mom and Dad are going to be thrilled," said Stardust. "Two horse-shoes in one day! Come on, let's go and get the other one and take them both back to the castle."

Stardust scooped up the horseshoe in her mouth and they returned to the stream. Pippa was so happy, she felt like she was walking on air. But as they drew nearer, they saw that Cinders was hunched up and crying. A cold feeling came over Pippa as she hurried toward her.

"Cinders, what's wrong?" she asked.

"I . . . I . . . I'm sorry," said Cinders. "It wasn't my fault. I only left it for a minute.

59

A foal came and told me that you needed me urgently, but I couldn't find you and when I came back the horseshoe was gone."

"What?" shrieked Stardust. "You left the horseshoe unguarded? How could you be so careless?"

Pippa was so shocked, it was as if all the breath had been squeezed out of her. But she knew that getting upset with Cinders wasn't going to help.

"We all make mistakes," she said kindly. "How long ago did it happen?"

A strange look crossed Cinders's face, and for a fleeting moment Pippa thought she almost smiled, but then Cinders's brown eyes seemed so full of remorse.

"Not long," Cinders answered.

Pippa realized that they had to be smart if they were to have any hope of recovering the horseshoe.

"Right, let's organize a search party," she decided.

She looked around to see who was available. Prince Storm, Prince Comet,

Trojan, and Mucker had come over to see what all the noise was about. But there was no time to organize them into proper groups, because Pippa saw something else.

At the far end of the field were two scruffy ponies who were behaving very strangely. They were sneaking away on hoof tips from the Grasslands. Pippa recognized them instantly.

"Night Mares," she said, pointing. "Although they're not Nightshade and Eclipse this time." Seeing something shiny, she added, "And they've stolen our horseshoe."

Stardust gave the fourth golden horseshoe to Mucker to keep safe.

"Quick," she shouted. "After them!"

Chapter 5

"Jump on!" Stardust turned around to stand by Pippa.

Grabbing a handful of mane, Pippa jumped onto Stardust's back. She was barely astride her when Stardust took off at a fast gallop. They were almost across the field when the Night Mares realized they'd been seen, and they took off with a whinny of surprise.

Storm and Comet had already

galloped off toward the Savannah, hoping to catch the Night Mares as they made their way back to the Volcano.

"Hurry," Pippa urged, leaning for ward like a jockey on a racing pony.

The mud was slowing Stardust down. Pippa could hear it squishing under her hooves, and some of it flicked up, splattering her own hands and face. Stardust struggled on, not caring about the mud, and slowly they began to catch up with the Night Mares.

"Go, Stardust!" Pippa yelled encouragingly.

"Hang on," Stardust shouted back. "I'm going to take a shortcut."

She changed direction, veering to the left and heading for a track. Pippa clutched Stardust's mane and gripped her flanks hard with her knees. She knew she had to concentrate on her balance. They couldn't risk losing sight of the Night Mares.

Pippa felt sick with excitement. If Stardust could keep this speed up, they would be able to cut the Night Mares off. She hunched low over Stardust's neck, her wavy brown hair flowing behind her.

Away to her left Pippa could hear a rattling noise. At first she ignored it, but the noise was growing steadily louder and was making Pippa uneasy. What was it? She looked around and gasped in horror. A cart, stacked high with cut grass and drawn by four enormous horses, was heading toward them. The stocky chestnut who was leading the horses hadn't noticed Stardust and Pippa, and at this rate Pippa knew they were all going to collide.

"Watch out, Stardust!" she screamed. "Cart to the left!"

Stardust turned her head, then slowed down in fright, unseating Pippa, who was forced to slide far up Stardust's neck.

"Sorry," Stardust said as she composed herself.

"Don't stop!" Pippa called, trying to push herself down Stardust's neck.

"But you might fall off," replied Stardust.

"I won't."

Gritting her teeth, Pippa clung on with all her strength. The ground raced by as Stardust's hooves carried them along at a frightening speed. If Pippa fell off now, Stardust might tread on her. Worse still, Pippa might even trip her friend up. She hung on tightly and pushed herself down Stardust's back. The cart was terrifyingly close.

"Out of the way!" Pippa screamed.

Frustration bubbled in her stomach. Couldn't the leading pony see the Night Mares and realize that they were chasing them? As they drew nearer, Pippa got a proper look at the leader. She recognized that square nose and those big eyes.

"Baroness Divine!"

The baroness didn't seem to notice the Night Mares and was smiling, apparently without a care in the world.

"What's she doing? Why is she here?" Stardust was confused. "She doesn't usually help with the harvest."

If they kept going, there would be a very nasty accident, so they had no

choice but to slow down. Snorting angrily, Stardust pawed the ground. They watched in frustration as the Night Mares galloped away.

"Afternoon," the baroness said, pulling up next to them. "My goodness, look at you both! Have you been having fun in the mud?"

Pippa eyed her suspiciously. It wasn't like the baroness to be so friendly.

"Yes, thank you, but we're too busy to stay and talk," Pippa replied.

Stardust darted behind the cart and broke into a gallop.

The Grasslands stretched ahead of them, flat and open, dotted with farm buildings, a forest in the distance. There was no sign of the Night Mares at all.

"They must be hiding," Stardust panted, dropping back to a canter. Her white coat was lathered with muddy sweat.

"Should I walk?" Pippa asked, running a hand down the pony's damp neck.

"I'm fine. We'll be quicker if you ride," Stardust said.

"Which way do you think they went?" Pippa asked as Stardust cantered on.

"It's got to be this way if they're going back to their home at the Volcano. We'll head toward the farm—it's the only place they can be hiding."

As the farm drew nearer, Stardust and Pippa whispered. Stardust placed her hooves carefully so that she was as quiet as possible.

"Over there," Pippa said suddenly,

"by the small barn—I saw something move."

Stardust switched direction. They'd almost reached the barn when there was a scuffling noise and the two Night Mares darted across the farmyard. One of them had the golden horseshoe in its mouth. Its eyes were wide with fear as it ran behind another barn.

"There!" called Stardust.

She chased after them but was too late—the Night Mares had disappeared.

Stardust stood very still, her ears swiveling as she tried to figure out where the Night Mares were hiding. Pippa listened too. At first all she could hear was her own heart pounding. Then a soft clatter grabbed her attention.

"Behind the grain store," she hissed.

Her stomach fluttered as Stardust went over to the building on hoof tips.

"Well, they're not here now," sighed Stardust.

Pippa stared in disbelief at the empty space. Some stones crunched behind her. Stardust turned around just in time for them to see the Night Mares run across the farmyard. The golden horse-shoe shone tantalizingly as they jumped over a fence and galloped away.

Chapter 6

"Hold on," said Stardust.

Pippa's hands shook as they cantered toward the fence. It was bigger than anything she'd jumped before. A shiver of fear ran down her spine. Stardust leaped at the jump. Just in time Pippa remembered to lift herself up off Stardust's back and grip with her knees. The wind whipped past her face and for a second she felt as if she was flying.

All her fears vanished—the jump felt fantastic. Then Stardust's front hooves hit the ground with a loud thud, and she raced after the Night Mares. The two scruffy ponies thundered on ahead, but they kept changing direction suddenly. Pippa quickly lost all sense of where she was. She was surprised when Stardust pulled up.

"Are you all right?" she asked.

"Yes," panted Stardust. "And I've had an idea. If we stop chasing the Night Mares, then they'll think we've given up and are heading home. I know another shortcut. I'm going to take it and hopefully we can cut them off."

"That's a brilliant idea," Pippa agreed.

Stardust waited for the Night Mares

to get totally out of sight so they wouldn't guess her plan. Once they'd disappeared, she headed into a nearby grove of trees. Pippa had to keep ducking her head to avoid being dragged off by low-hanging branches. Bushes and twigs snagged her legs as they hammered along the narrow path and jumped the fallen logs blocking their way. It was almost fun, but Pippa thought it didn't seem right to be enjoying the ride when there was so much at stake.

"Nearly there," Stardust called. "I just hope we've made it in time."

"Me too," said Pippa.

They burst out of the woods and into a clearing, where Trojan and a group of

ponies were lifting the newly harvested rectangular bales of grass from an open-topped cart and arranging them into an enormous haystack. There were snorts of alarm as Stardust pulled up, and work stopped immediately.

"What is going on?" A proud voice cut across the commotion.

"Crystal!" cried Stardust. Lowering her voice so that only Pippa could hear, she added, "I never thought I'd be so pleased to see her."

"Princess Stardust, why aren't you out in the fields picking up grass?" Crystal glared at her little sister and then at Pippa.

Stardust quickly explained how they had found two of the golden horseshoes and then how the Night Mares had stolen one back.

"I see," said Crystal. She took charge at once. "If the Night Mares see us here they'll run away, so everyone must hide in the trees. I'll wait behind this haystack and challenge them when they arrive. As next in line to the throne of

Chevalia, I'm sure they'll give me the horseshoe when I ask for it back——"

"But I thought——" interrupted Stardust.

Crystal gave her a steely glare. "Don't argue. I'm older than you."

"That's so typical of Crystal. We do all the hard work and she takes the glory," Stardust grumbled as she went to hide with the other ponies.

"It's very brave of her to challenge the Night Mares on her own," Pippa pointed out.

"Or stupid," Stardust said angrily. "Sometimes Crystal doesn't think things through. What happens if the Night Mares refuse to give her the horseshoe?"

"Then we're here to help," Pippa

replied, running a comforting hand down Stardust's neck. "She didn't tell *us* to stay hidden, did she?"

Stardust whinnied with laughter, then instantly fell silent as Trojan sent her a stern look and said, "Sssh."

Pippa and Stardust hid in the trees a little distance from Trojan and waited. When the Night Mares didn't arrive, Pippa wondered if Stardust had been mistaken and they'd gone another way. She tried not to think about the three days left until Midsummer. If only the magic time bubble could stop time in Chevalia too! She'd stop it right now and only start it again when they'd found all the missing horseshoes.

Suddenly Stardust threw up her head. Her ears twitched, then swiveled to the right.

"Night Mares," she whispered softly.

In the distance Pippa could hear the drumming of hooves. She shivered with excitement. This was their chance to grab the golden horseshoe. They couldn't mess it up.

As the Night Mares ran closer, Pippa saw that they were being chased by a swarm of angry horseflies.

"You tricked ussss," buzzed the horseflies. "Now give the golden horseshoe back to usss."

The Night Mares were scared. Their eyes were wild and their nostrils flared as they approached the clearing.

"Where's Crystal?" said Stardust. "She's supposed to challenge them. If she doesn't hurry up, it'll be too late."

"There she is." Pippa pointed as Crystal's head cautiously appeared around the side of the haystack, then quickly disappeared as she pulled back again.

"Oh no!" gasped Stardust. "I get it now. Crystal is scared of horseflies."

"Then it's up to us," Pippa replied.

Up close the Night Mares were frightening to look at, with wild eyes, straggly manes and tails, and bodies covered in gray volcanic ash. Stardust shook for just a moment before bravely stepping out of the woods and into their path.

"Stop!" she commanded. "Give the golden horseshoe back to us."

"Never!" the Night Mares shrieked, rearing up.

Stardust stood her ground as the Night Mares came closer, still pursued by the angry horseflies. Pippa was terrified that she and Stardust were about to be run down, and her knuckles whitened as she clutched Stardust's mane.

The Night Mares were so close that she could see the whites of their eyes and feel their hot breath flecked with spit. Her eyes watered at the bad smell that wafted toward her.

At the last moment the Night Mares neighed angrily, then changed course. In their hurry, one of them backed into Stardust, hitting Pippa's leg. Pippa winced but there was no time to examine the damage. The Night Mare with the horseshoe in its mouth was close enough for her to touch. Pippa reached out and grabbed it.

"No, it's mine," the Night Mare grunted, trying to tug it out of Pippa's grasp.

Pippa refused to let go, twisting her body so that she could keep hold of the horseshoe as Stardust turned around to kick into the air to scare the other Night Mare away. Pippa could feel herself slipping, but she held on tightly to the horseshoe, blinking back tears when a tail flicked in her eye.

The Night Mares shoved Stardust sideways. Pippa was dimly aware of Stardust grunting as she pushed them back and Crystal whinnying for everyone to stop. Stardust was barely holding her ground, until together the two Night Mares forced her toward the haystack. The horseflies buzzed angrily overhead.

Everything seemed to happen in slow motion. Pippa felt as if she was watching herself in a film as the haystack loomed right in front of her. There was an ominous creak, and then it was raining bales of hay. Pippa covered her head with her hands and gritted her teeth as she willed the avalanche to stop. But a hay bale whacked into Pippa and knocked her off Stardust. The next thing Pippa knew, she was being flung through the air.

Chapter 7

Pippa was lucky that she only fell onto a pile of hay rather than a hay bale. She lay on her back, grateful for such a soft landing, listening to the thundering hooves of the retreating Night Mares as the horseflies chased them away. A tall wall of rectangular hay bales towered above her—the only part of the haystack that remained. The rest of it littered the ground in messy clumps. She looked down at her hand and saw that she was still clutching the horseshoe.

"Look! I've still got the horseshoe," Pippa said, struggling up.

"Well done." Stardust had managed to stay upright, but she looked slightly dazed.

"Just look at the mess!" said Crystal,

who had narrowly missed being hit by the avalanche of hay. "We've been working on this haystack all day."

Pippa started to laugh—trust Crystal to worry about the mess when they'd just managed to rescue a horseshoe! She wrapped her arms around Stardust's hot neck.

"You were fantastic," Pippa said, hugging her.

"So were you," Stardust said proudly. "Mom and Dad are never going to believe us when we tell them what happened."

"They'll be absolutely thrilled!" said Pippa.

The ponies filed out of the woods led by Trojan. When they saw Pippa holding the golden horseshoe, their eyes widened and they whinnied excitedly.

"Are you all right?" Jet asked.

"What happened?" asked Comet.

"Pippa snatched it back from a Night Mare," boasted Stardust.

"Stardust and Crystal helped," Pippa said quickly.

Trojan sent Crystal such a look of admiration that it made her blush.

"Actually, I didn't do anything," she said. "It was all Stardust and Pippa's work."

Trojan was even more impressed that Crystal had been honest and not taken any of the credit, especially when it was offered to her. He softly brushed his nose against hers.

Crystal blushed so deeply that even the blaze on her apricot-colored face turned red. She shyly rubbed her nose against Trojan's, causing him to blush too.

"Aw! Sweet," Stardust whispered to her friend.

"Stop staring." Pippa giggled, pulling

her around. Every single one of Pippa's muscles ached, but she didn't care.

The horseflies returned, having chased the Night Mares far away.

"Thank you so much for all your help," said Crystal. "And I'm sorry I never took the time to listen to you before."

"Come back to the castle with us," Stardust said.

Zimb shook his head politely. "Our work isss done here," he buzzed, bowing low. "We're sssorry we caused you ssssso much trouble. In the future we will send a team of horsefliessss to guard the horseshoessss hanging on the ancient wall."

"Thank you," Stardust said gratefully.

"I'll have to ask Mom and Dad about it first, but it sounds like a brilliant idea."

The horseflies swarmed off, and Pippa, Stardust, Crystal, Trojan, and the princes walked back to the stream. By now the news had spread that two more horseshoes were safe, and as they walked through the Grasslands more ponies joined them.

Mucker was still guarding the other horseshoe and looked very impressed when Stardust and Pippa made their triumphant return.

"What happened to keeping clean?" he asked.

Stardust blushed prettily. "There's nothing wrong with a bit of muck and a good day's work," she answered. "We're taking the two horseshoes back to the castle to hang them on the ancient wall." Then she added, "In fact, everyone's invited."

An excited murmur rippled through the gathering of ponies. Cinders pushed herself to the front of the crowd.

"You can't appear in the Royal Court like that," she said. "Look how dirty you are! Give me the horseshoes. I'm clean—I'll take them back."

A cunning look flashed across her face, but it was gone so quickly that Pippa decided she must have imagined it.

"No, thanks," said Stardust. "Pippa and I did all the work. We're not letting you take the glory. We'll hang the horse-shoes ourselves."

"It's true—you *are* very dirty," said Crystal.

"We promise to be careful," Pippa said. "And we won't get the horseshoes muddy."

Crystal looked thoughtful. "Maybe it's time I lightened up a bit and was less proud and bossy."

She glanced at Trojan and a pink flush crept up her neck. Trojan was flushing too. Stardust nudged Pippa's arm and they giggled together. Crystal quickly recovered her composure.

"You can take the horseshoes back to the castle," Crystal said. "Then afterward I'm treating you both to a luxury session at the Mane Street Salon. You deserve some serious pampering. Pippa, ask for

the strawberry mane wash—I think you'll love it."

"Thank you," Pippa said. "That sounds wonderful."

Stardust turned to face the crowd. "So who's coming to the Royal Court with us?"

"Me! And me!" all of Canter's whinnied excitedly.

Side by side and both clutching a golden horseshoe, Pippa and Stardust led the procession back to Stableside Castle. Pippa's muscles still ached and she felt very tired, but extremely happy.

It took a while to get back and even longer for everyone to crowd into the ancient courtyard. All the prince and princess ponies lined up together to

watch. Queen Moonshine and King Firestar smiled proudly at Stardust and Pippa as they made their way to the Whispering Wall.

Cinders stood next to her mom, Baroness Divine, at the front of the crowd.

"There goes Princess Grunge," she said meanly.

Dipping her square face, the baroness whispered to Cinders, "The Royal Family has definitely lowered its standards."

Pippa didn't hear Cinders's answer but Baroness Divine chuckled quietly and whispered, "That's right, my dear. Things will soon be different in Chevalia."

The menace in her voice gave Pippa goose bumps. What did the baroness mean? But there was no time to think about it now. Reaching the queen, Pippa bowed her head and forced her aching legs into a low curtsy.

The queen lightly touched the top of Pippa's head with her nose. As Pippa stood up, she saw that there were tears in her beautiful dark eyes.

"Pippa MacDonald, you are truly a very special girl. You've worked hard today and weren't afraid to get your hands dirty. You were also very brave. Chevalia salutes you."

To Pippa's embarrassment, everyone cheered.

"Thank you, but I didn't do it on my own. Stardust helped, and the horseflies, and Mucker and Crystal," Pippa added generously.

"Hush, child," the queen said, smiling.

First Stardust and then Pippa handed a golden horseshoe to the king, who carefully hung them on the Whispering Wall. He stood back to admire them, and the crowd cheered again.

The wall didn't look so empty with four horseshoes hanging there, but Pippa was very conscious that time was running out. There were only three more days before Midsummer. Would they find all the missing horseshoes? The days ahead would be difficult and dangerous, but Pippa felt ready. Chevalia needed her more than ever.

"Congratulations," said Queen Moonshine. Then, as if echoing Pippa's thoughts, she added, "However, your quest isn't over. Midsummer Day will soon be here, and there are still four horseshoes to find. Go safely, my children, and please remember—don't count your horseshoes before they're hung!"

"Thank you, Your Majesty—and we won't," said Pippa.

Stardust reached out and nuzzled Pippa's arm.

"To Chevalia," she whispered.

"To Chevalia," Pippa replied softly.

Chevalia Now!

**EXCLUSIVE
INTERVIEW WITH
MUCKER**

by Tulip Inkhoof

There's no doubt that this Harvest Day will go down as the busiest one in Chevalia's history. Reporter Tulip Inkhoof caught up with Mucker, the youngest farm pony, for an eyewitness account of all today's action over in the Grasslands.

☆ **TI (Tulip Inkhoof):** Thanks for agreeing to speak to me, Mucker. May I just ask that you wash your horseshoes before we start the interview?

☆ **M (Mucker):** But I'm proud of my muddy hooves! Getting dirty and working hard are as much a part of Harvest Day as the picnic lunch.

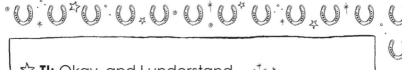

TI: Okay, and I understand that even the Royal Family enjoys mucking about on the farm?

M: Stardust certainly does— she always helps out. In fact, she works so hard and gets so muddy that Cinders calls her Princess Grunge.

TI: Was it a shock to learn that there were two golden horseshoes hidden in the grass?

M: Yes, I couldn't believe it! The grass was growing really tall even though it hadn't rained, and we were beginning to wonder why. Thanks to Zimb and the horseflies, we discovered it was because of the magic from the golden horseshoes.

☆ **TI:** Talking horseflies indeed! Did you know they could communicate with you?

☆ **M:** I had no idea! I've batted away plenty of horseflies and never once did I think that they were trying to talk to me. It just goes to show that you don't truly understand someone until you've listened to them properly.

☆ **TI:** And I hear that the Night Mares stole a horseshoe almost as soon as it was discovered? How dramatic!

4

☆ **M:** Yes, Pippa and Stardust had just found the fourth missing horseshoe when two Night Mares came out of nowhere and snatched the horseshoe that Cinders was supposed to be guarding. Pippa gave me her horseshoe for safekeeping, then she and Stardust chased after the Night Mares.

5

They were so
brave, and
Trojan
was really
impressed
with Crystal
too!

☆ **TI:** Thanks for filling me in, Mucker. Now I suggest that you really do find a water trough and get cleaned up!

Will Pippa and Princess Stardust find all the golden horseshoes?

DON'T MISS THEIR NEXT ADVENTURE IN THE CLOUD FOREST!

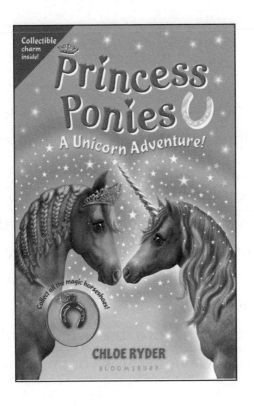

Turn the page to read a sneak peek . . .

As Pippa got up, she remembered something important—Chevalia existed in a magical bubble. No time would pass in her world while she was on the island, meaning that none of her family would miss her. Pippa's homesickness vanished immediately.

She skipped to the window to see where the singing was coming from.

Princess Stardust's bedroom was in the smallest tower of the castle, topped with a pink flag, and it had a marvelous view. Pippa glanced at the sea sparkling in the distance before looking at the courtyard below.

"It's the Royal Court," she breathed.

All the ponies of the Royal Court were gathered together, with the princesses and princes in the front. Their colorful sashes and jeweled tiaras shimmered in the morning sun. Crystal, Stardust's bossy oldest sister, was conducting the singing with a riding crop, and the music made Pippa want to dance. When she had first arrived on Chevalia, Pippa had been so shy, but now she was starting to feel as if she belonged here and she couldn't wait to join them.

Pippa quickly put on the new outfit that had magically appeared overnight especially for her—a denim skirt, a striped T-shirt, leggings, and a sweat-shirt—then she hurried down the tower's spiral ramp.

"Excuse me," she whispered as she made her way to the front of the court-yard. The royal ponies smiled as they parted to let her through. "Thanks," she said.

Princess Honey was singing next to Stardust, tapping the ground in time to the music with a sparkly pink hoof. She was very pretty, with a shiny, straw-berry chestnut coat, but she couldn't quite reach the higher notes, and her voice kept squeaking.

"You sound like a rusty stable door," Stardust said, laughing at her.

Honey hung her head.

"Hi, Stardust. Hi, Honey," Pippa whispered, squeezing between them. "What's going on?"

"We're rehearsing for the Royal Concert," Stardust replied. "We always hold it on Midsummer Day, to give thanks for Chevalia and the magical horseshoes. But Honey won't be allowed to sing if she keeps on making that racket." She playfully nudged her older sister.

Honey's brown eyes filled with tears. "You're so mean!" she said. Pushing past Stardust, she trotted out of the courtyard.

"There isn't going to be a concert if we don't find the horseshoes," said Pippa. "But before we start searching for them, you'd better find Honey and say sorry for hurting her feelings."

Stardust was surprised. "I was only teasing. I didn't mean to upset her—I forgot how much she wanted to sing the solo."

Stardust was anxious to make it up to her sister, so together they sneaked out of the Royal Courtyard.

Once outside, she whinnied to Pippa, "Get on my back."

Pippa jumped onto Stardust's snowy white back, and they cantered off to look for Honey.